Hey Jack! Books

First American Edition 2023
Kane Miller, A Division of EDC Publishing

Text copyright © 2022 Sally Rippin
Illustration copyright © 2022 Stephanie Spartels
Series design copyright © 2023 Hardie Grant Children's Publishing
Original Title: Hey Jack!: *The Backyard Mystery*
First published in Australia by Hardie Grant Children's Publishing

For information contact:
Kane Miller, A Division of EDC Publishing
5402 S 122nd E Ave
Tulsa, OK 74146
www.kanemiller.com

Library of Congress Control Number: 2022945489
Printed and bound in the United States of America
1 2 3 4 5 6 7 8 9 10

ISBN: 978-1-68464-666-1

Hey Jack!

The Backyard Mystery

By Sally Rippin

Illustrated by Stephanie Spartels

Kane Miller
A DIVISION OF EDC PUBLISHING

Big thoughts

Mom's laptop

Learning Mood

Chapter One

This is Jack. Today
Jack is busy studying.
He is learning about
insects. Insects are so
interesting!

His favorite insect is the butterfly.

"OK, Jack," his mom says. "Off the computer now. I need it for work."

"Can we go to the zoo?" Jack asks. "I really want to go and see the butterflies!"

"Maybe tomorrow," his mom says. "I have to work today. How about you go outside and play?"

Jack runs outside. He **flitters** all around the backyard. Just like a beautiful butterfly.

Jack's best friend, Billie, lives next door. She pokes her head through a gap in the fence.

"What are you playing?"
Billie asks.

"Butterflies!" says Jack.
He **flaps** his arms up
and down.

Billie squeezes through
the hole in the fence.
"Can I play?" she says.

"Sure!" says Jack.

Billie runs around after Jack. She flaps her arms up and down. Then she starts snapping them. Snap! Snap! **Snap!**

"I'm a crocodile!" she says. She **snaps** at Jack with her big crocodile mouth.

"Ow!" says Jack. "You are meant to be a butterfly, Billie!"

Billie giggles. "Butterflies are boring!" she growls. "I want to be a lion!"

"We always play what you want," Jack says. He feels cross.

Billie is his best friend in the whole world. But sometimes she can be a teensy bit bossy.

"I don't want to play lions," he says. "I want to play butterflies!"

Billie frowns. She **flops** down on the grass.

Jack flops down next to her. He doesn't like it when they argue.

"I know," he says. "How about we play flying lions? Half butterfly, half lion?"

"Yeah!" says Billie.

They jump up.

Jack **chases** Billie around the backyard. They flap their arms and roar very loudly.

Jack's mom pops her head out the back door. "Kids!" she says. "That's too loud!"

"But we are **flying lions!**" Jack says. "Lions are always noisy!"

"Can you be quiet lions, please?" Jack's mom asks.

"I have to work!" She

goes back inside.

"Quiet lions?" Jack

giggles. "There's no such

thing! Let's be **frogs**

instead. We can look for

insects to eat."

"Good idea!" says Billie.

She hops around the garden. Jack follows her. "Ribbit! Ribbit! Ribbit!"

Jack sees something stuck to a leaf. He stops hopping. "Billie!" he gasps. "Look! A cocoon!"

Chapter Two

Billie pokes at the cocoon with her finger.

"Careful!" says Jack. "It might have a butterfly inside." He smiles.

"I'm going to take it to my room. We can watch it hatch."

"How long will that take?" Billie frowns.

Jack shrugs. "I don't know," he says.

"That sounds boring," Billie says.

17

"No, it's not!" says Jack. "Butterflies are **amazing!**"

"I think I'll go home," Billie says. "Call me when the butterfly is here."

Billie climbs back through the hole in the fence.

Jack feels **annoyed** that Billie isn't excited about the cocoon. Maybe his mom will like it?

He carries the cocoon inside on its leaf.

"Mom, look what I found!" Jack says. "A cocoon!"

"That's great, darling!" Jack's mom says. She smiles at Jack. Then she looks back at her computer screen.

No one seems to be as interested in the cocoon as he is.

Jack goes upstairs
with the cocoon.
He finds an old shoebox
in his bedroom.
He puts the cocoon
inside. Then he fills
the box with twigs
and leaves from the
backyard.

"This is your new home,
little butterfly!" he says.

"You are going to **love** it here!"

Jack watches the cocoon all afternoon. He watches it all evening. He eats dinner quickly so he can go back and watch the cocoon again.

He can't wait for it to hatch!

Jack **imagines** what the butterfly will look like. He hopes it is blue. Blue butterflies are his favorite.

Jack's dad stands in the doorway. "Time for bed, Jack!" he says.

"I can't go to bed now, Dad!" Jack says. "I might miss the butterfly!"

Jack's dad smiles. "Don't worry," he says. "Butterflies only come out in the day. It will still be there tomorrow."

Jack snuggles down into bed.

He dreams that he
and Billie are beautiful
butterflies. They fly all
around the backyard.

Chapter Three

The next morning,
Jack runs downstairs for
breakfast.

"Sorry I was so busy
yesterday," his mom says.

"I have finished my work now. Shall we go to the zoo today?"

Jack feels **worried**. "Oh, I'd love to. But I don't want to miss my butterfly! It might come out today."

"Are you sure?" says Jack's mom. "You can invite Billie, too."

Jack doesn't know what to do. He really wants to go to the zoo with his mom and Billie.

But he doesn't want to miss seeing the butterfly hatch.

Jack thinks hard.

"I know!" he says.

30

"Can I borrow your computer, Mom? I will see how long it takes for a cocoon to hatch. Then I will know if we can go to the zoo today."

"Of course!" says his mom. "What a good idea."

Jack looks up cocoons on the internet. They are all different shapes and sizes. None of them look like his cocoon!

Hmmm … That's a bit strange, he thinks.

But then Jack sees
a cocoon that looks
exactly like his.

Uh-oh!

Jack's heart starts beating
faster. That's not a
butterfly cocoon in
his bedroom. That's a
spider's egg sac!

Jack's mom is **scared** of spiders. She always asks Jack to catch them and take them outside.

Imagine if there was a whole family of them inside!

He has to get that cocoon out of the house. And fast!

Jack **rushes** upstairs.
He opens his door and
peers into his room.

Phew! It looks like he's not too late. No spiders to be seen.

Jack carefully carries the box downstairs. He walks to the very end of the backyard.

Billie pokes her head through the gap in the fence. "What are you doing?" she says.

Jack lifts out the leaf with the egg sac stuck to it.

"Billie," he says quietly. He doesn't want his mom to hear. "It's not a butterfly in there! It's **baby spiders**! A whole lot of them!"

"Ew!" says Billie. She runs over to look.

"Spiders are scary!"

"Nah. Spiders are awesome," says Jack. "They won't hurt you if you leave them alone. But it's better if they live in the backyard. Not my bedroom!" He puts the leaf on the ground.

"Lucky you were watching," Billie says. She looks **impressed**. "Imagine if baby spiders had hatched in your room!"

"I know!" Jack laughs. "Hey, do you want to come with me to the zoo today? Mom said she'll take us."

"Yes, please!" says Billie.
"We can go and see the
lions! And the elephants!"

41

She **roars** loudly, swinging her arm like a trunk. "Elephants are my favorite!"

Jack frowns.

Billie sees his face and laughs. "I'm sorry, Jack," Billie says. "We'll go and see your favorite, too."

Read them all!

 Hey Jack! The Crazy Cousins By Sally Rippin

 Hey Jack! The Scary Solo By Sally Rippin

 Hey Jack! The Winning Goal By Sally Rippin

 Hey Jack! The Robot Blues By Sally Rippin

 Hey Jack! The Worry Monster By Sally Rippin

 Hey Jack! The New Friend By Sally Rippin

 Hey Jack! The Worst Sleepover By Sally Rippin

 Hey Jack! The Circus Lesson By Sally Rippin

 Hey Jack! The Bumpy Ride By Sally Rippin

 Hey Jack! The Top Team By Sally Rippin

 Hey Jack! The Playground Problem By Sally Rippin

 Hey Jack! The Best Party Ever By Sally Rippin

 Hey Jack! The Bravest Kid By Sally Rippin

 Hey Jack! The Big Adventure By Sally Rippin

 Hey Jack! The Toy Sale By Sally Rippin

 Hey Jack! The Star of the Week By Sally Rippin

 Hey Jack! The Extra-special Group By Sally Rippin

 Hey Jack! The Other Teacher By Sally Rippin

 Hey Jack! The Party Invite By Sally Rippin

 Hey Jack! The Lost Reindeer By Sally Rippin

 Hey Jack! The Backyard Mystery By Sally Rippin

 Hey Jack! The Special Guest By Sally Rippin

And don't forget the book starring both Jack and Billie!

 Billie B Brown & Hey Jack! The Book Buddies By Sally Rippin